The Perfect Present

Stella J Jones • Caroline Pedler

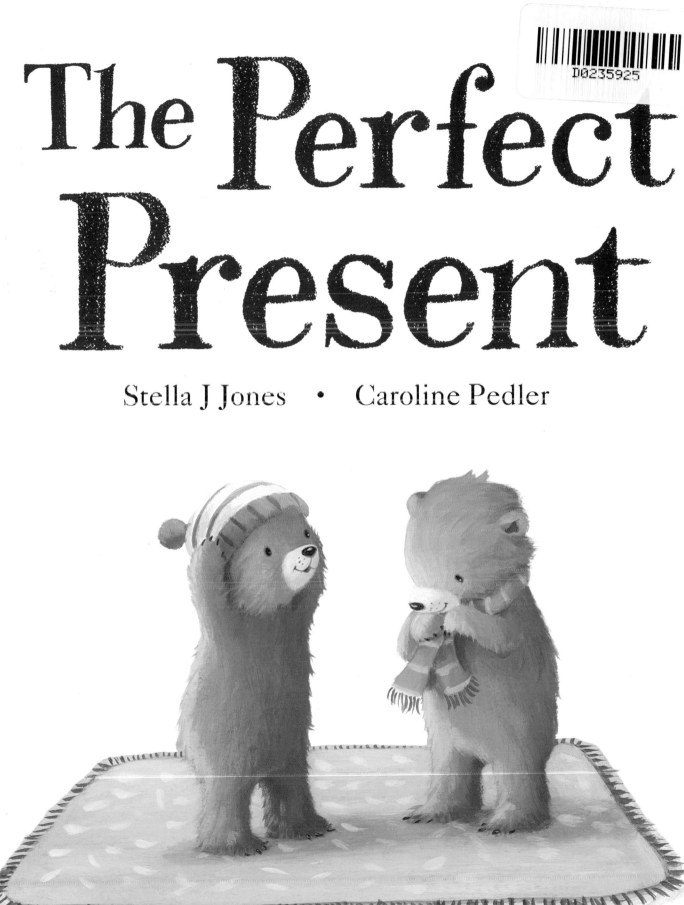

LITTLE TIGER PRESS
London

It was nearly Christmas and the village was
all a-twinkle with tinsel and lights.

"This is the BEST time of year!" cheered Billy,
whizzing along on his scooter.

"Faster, faster!" called Bella, pedalling up beside him.
"Or we'll miss the Christmas tree lights!"

"Three, two, one, hooray!" everyone cried as the tree sparkled into life.

"One more sleep till Santa comes!" smiled Bella, squeezing Billy's paw.

"One last day for Christmas shopping!"
grinned Billy. "See you later!"
    He hopped on his scooter and rushed off
to buy Bella the perfect gift.

The shelves at Hattie Hardwick's shop were choc-a-block with beautiful things, but nothing was just right for Bella.

"Bother," sighed Billy.

Then something bright red caught his eye.

"A flag for Bella's trike!" he gasped. "That's exactly the thing that Bella would like best."

We SWAP OLD for NEW!

But there weren't enough pennies
in Billy's purse.

"Oh no!" he fretted. "What should I do?"

"Don't worry," said Hattie gently. "Is there something you'd like to swap for the flag?"

Billy thought hard and looked down at his battered scooter. Could he possibly part with it?

"I can swap this," he said bravely, handing the scooter to Hattie.

"Bella will love her present," Billy told himself as he looked up at his scooter in the window.

But he couldn't help feeling a little bit sad
as he padded slowly home through the
crowds of Christmas shoppers.

Across town, it didn't take Bella long to find the
perfect present for Billy.

"That's it!" she cried, staring at the brightest,
shiniest bell in the shop window. "I'll get Billy
that bell for his scooter."

She rushed into the shop,
but she didn't have enough
pennies either!

"This is truly terrible,"
thought Bella.

NEW
for OLD!
Why not
SWAP?

Suddenly she spotted a sign behind
the counter. It said:

New for old! Why not swap?

"What could I give?" Bella pondered.
Then she had an idea. "I can swap
my trike!" she told the shopkeeper.

Bella sniffed a sorry sniff as she left
her trusty trike behind.

But she soon cheered up when she
thought about how much Billy would
love his bell.

After they'd warmed up with Christmas cocoa, the friends raced off to wrap their gifts.

"You're going to love your present!" called Billy as he snipped and folded the wrapping paper.

"Not as much as you'll like yours!" replied Bella, tying a bow.

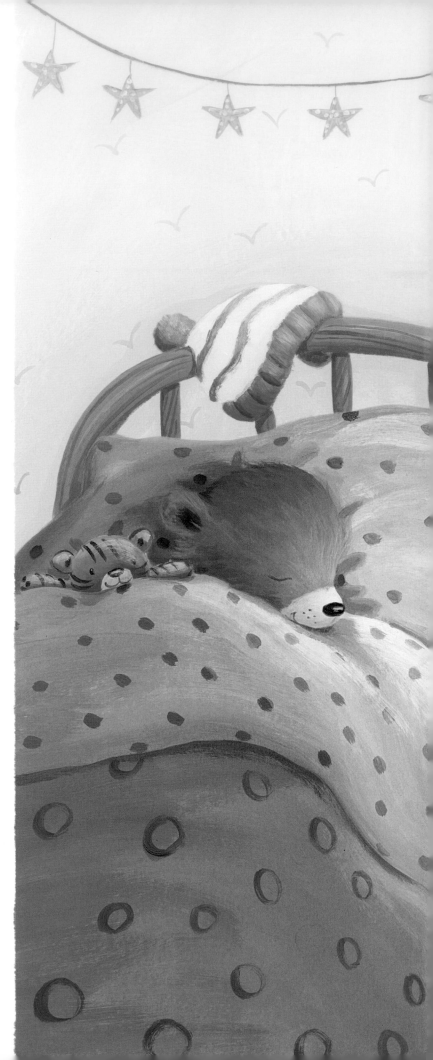

But as they slept, scooters and trikes whooshed and whizzed through their dreams – and they were always just out of reach.

"Happy Christmas!" Billy and Bella cried merrily
as the sun peeped through the curtains.
    "Ready?" asked Billy.
    "Steady!" cried Bella.
    "Unwrap!" they shouted together.

Billy couldn't believe his eyes!

"A bell for my scooter!" he gasped.

"And a flag for my trike!" squealed Bella.

"This is the best present ever!"

And then they remembered . . .

"But I swapped my scooter for your flag," sniffed Billy.
"And I swapped my trike for your bell!" gulped Bella.

Bella gave Billy a hug.
"I don't mind that I don't have my trike," she said. "I still have you."

"You really are the best friend ever," smiled Billy.
They both began to giggle. "What a pair we are!"

"Let's open our presents from Santa," suggested Billy. "That will cheer us up."

He reached under the tree and pulled out two packages. There was a note which read:

Dear Billy and Bella,
I know what kind and thoughtful friends you have both been, so my elves have been working on something very special for you.
Merry Christmas!
Love, Santa

"Whatever could it be?" wondered Bella as she tore off the paper.

"I don't believe it!" she exclaimed. "It's . . . it's my trike!"

"And look! My scooter!" added Billy. "It's as good as new! Thank you, Santa!"

With the bell and flag in place, there was only
one thing left to do.

   "Race you to the pond and back!"
called Bella happily.

   "Ready, steady, GO!" laughed Billy.
And the friends rushed out into the crisp Christmas day.